The Poetic Choice Of A Black Voice

Samantha Rodgers

Book cover design by
Samah Al Ansari

My voice yearns for an audience.
It demands to be heard,
Unfiltered, undiluted,
Cohesive not slurred.
My words crave for empathy.
They are not here to offend.
But my voice is powerful.
It echoes with no end.

Samantha Rodgers

www.nubianamedia.com

CONTENTS

Those

To those who stood before us.
To those who paid the price,
To fight for our freedom.
We respect your sacrifice.

To those who are still fighting.
To those who still campaign.
To those trying to eradicate racism,
May your fighting spirit remain.

To those who have been courageous.
To those who have been bold.
To those who have used their voices,
To expose injustices untold.

To those who bravely rebelled.
To those who died in pain.
You will always be our heroes,
Your efforts will never be in vain.

Still

Still we stand,
After all we've been through,
So many things,
That we can't undo.
So many wrongs,
That have been committed,
Allowed to happen,
And lawfully permitted.

Yet still we stand,
Protesting for our rights.
Not waiting for permission,
But being prepared to fight,
For the sakes of our children,
So they can have more,
Not destined to experience,
Things we had to endure.

Our History

So much of our history
Has not been told,
Instead a false narrative,
Has deviously been sold.
Raised in a world
That conveniently told lies,
In order to erase our history.
Hiding the truth from our eyes.

History has been whitewashed
To give a false portrayal,
Diminishing our story
The ultimate betrayal.
Instead led to believe
That we had no worth,
Even though we derive from greatness,
The first people of the earth.

Our history has been distorted
To hide their treacherous ways,
While they rewrote the past
And showered themselves with praise.
Delusional about their heroes
Whilst covering up their crimes.
Erecting statues in their honour
Forgetting evil, ruthless times.

Proud of their invasions
They gained control of many lands,
Brainwashing the natives
With a bible in their hands.
So while our history has been sidelined,
Pushed aside, right to the back,
It's no wonder why some of us
Have no pride in being black.

Enslaved

Our journey did not begin with slavery,
We did not start off in chains.
There were glorious tribes in Africa,
Before slavery inflicted its pain.

The birthplace of civilisation.
Ancient kingdoms, strong and united.
Living without inferiority,
Until the oppressor arrived uninvited.

Ripped away from our culture.
Stolen from our ancestral land.
Bought and sold like cattle,
By ruthless greedy hands.

We were captured and enslaved.
Not simply born as slaves.
As our ancestors perished,
In the ocean's shallow graves.

They banished our beloved traditions.
They replaced our African names.
Life in the Motherland,
Would never be the same.

This is part of our painful history,
It hurts with deep wounds of regret,
But we did not commence as slaves,
Let us never ever forget.

Rebellion

Never let it be told,
That we did not rebel.
We fought against slavery.
The story they rarely tell.
We fought for our emancipation.
We fought to be free.
We fought for our survival,
To be treated with dignity.

Our ancestors were warriors,
They rebelled and they tried,
To break our chains of slavery,
From the battle they did not hide.
Be proud of your ancestors.
Be proud of their non-compliance.
Be proud of their determination.
Be proud of their defiance.

It is easy to depict us,
As victims with no fight,
But the rebels were no pushover,
They rebelled with all of their might.
They did more than just protest,
The truth they've withheld.
We stood up against our oppressors,
With force we rebelled.

Rise

We rise by lifting others,
So it's imperative to understand,
We can support one another,
By lending a helping hand.

We can all make a difference.
We can all motivate
Another person in this world,
Helping them to navigate.

Everyone needs a hero,
Someone who inspires,
And gives us courage,
To pursue our deepest desires.

We owe all we have,
To people who took a chance,
To chase their dreams.
Now our lives are enhanced.

Our ancestors took the first steps,
Into the daunting unknown,
So now it's our opportunity,
To be a trailblazer of our own.

Windrush

As the Windrush ship approached,
Docking on British shores.
Many dreamed of a better life,
The opportunity to achieve much more.
They excitedly clambered gown the steps,
With their suitcases in hand,
Ready to embark on a journey,
In this assumed prestigious land.

They left the Caribbean,
In search of prospects and gold,
But it was not the promise,
Of which they had been told.
Believing they would be welcomed,
With warm inviting hands,
Arriving to their sovereign's home,
A supposed prosperous land.

Welcomed by a bitter wind,
A coldness so unknown.
They longed to see the sunshine,
And yearned to go back home.
Prejudice and discrimination,
Surrounded them everywhere.
Only the brave could survive.
Only the brave would dare.

Signs were openly posted,
In order to segregate.
NO blacks! NO dogs! NO Irish!
Used to discriminate.
Life was not easy.
Equality was simply a word.
This was not the land they expected,
To which they had been lured.

Imported for their labour,
A mass wave of immigration.
Paving the way for their children.
The brave Windrush generation.

United

The plan was very easy.
To make us fight within,
So while we are divided,
They control us and then win.

We've fallen for the rhetoric.
We've fallen for the lies.
We've fallen for self-hatred,
While we walk with blinded eyes.

If we stand united,
And really work together,
Our union will be solidified,
Bonded tight forever.

It's time to stand as one,
And stop being short-sighted.
Our battle still lies ahead.
But we're stronger when united.

The Field

It’s never been equal,
It’s never been fair.
A head start for some,
And for others, no care.
One rule for us,
One rule for them,
Allowances for others,
While some are condemned.

Some given privilege,
An unfair advantage,
While others are blocked,
By a clear disadvantage.
Judged for no reason,
Under constant suspicion,
While others are carefree,
In beneficial positions.

Preferential treatment,
For some still remains,
Leaving others to suffer,
With very little gain.
The field is not level,
The messages are mixed.
They’ll never be justice,
Until it is fixed.

Africa

Astonishing amazing Africa.
A continent so beautiful and grand,
With a long diverse history,
That many misunderstand.
With over fifty different countries,
And a wide range of languages spoken,
Africa is not a singular place.
Such ignorance needs to be broken.

Often portrayed as impoverished,
In order to achieve
A distorted view of Africa,
So that many will believe
That it has no real value,
But we know that's not the case,
Which is why it's always exploited,
Because it's such a lucrative place.

Rich in natural resources,
Like diamonds, copper and gold.
The greedy rush to Africa,
To buy what can be sold.
Making profits from the land,
And taking from African soil,
The reserves that lie deep down beneath,
Especially the gas and oil.

So please don't judge Africa,
By the warped images you view on TV.
It is a magnificent continent,
With so many wonders to see.
It is our original birthplace,
Of this you can’t refute,
So let’s all embrace Africa,
And be proud our ancestral roots.

Wakanda

Wakanda, Wakanda.
I wish you were real.
This wonderful nation,
Would be so surreal.

We are innovative people,
With so many skills on hand,
To return to a new Wakanda,
And invest in the Motherland.

To rebuild centuries of ruin.
To inspire future generations.
It's time for a momentous,
Homecoming celebration.

Wakanda, Wakanda.
A land of which I yearn.
I'd buy a one-way ticket.
No need for a return.

Reflection

When you look in the mirror,
Look carefully at your reflection.
The person that you see,
Has your ancestors' protection.
It is not only you
But all those who stood before,
Who made many sacrifices,
And have opened many doors,
For you to walk through,
Making your journey much lighter,
To embark on a future,
That is ultimately brighter.

You are stronger than you think.
You reflect so much power.
You are braver every day,
Every minute, every hour.
So embrace your reflection,
And have belief in your dreams,
With your ancestors' spirits,
It is easier than it seems.
So never allow others,
To cast their negative projections,
Or dim your shining light,
Have faith in your reflection.

They Say

They say it happened years ago.
They say it was a terrible shame.
They say that it was their ancestors,
So they are not to blame.
They say there's no need for reparations.
They say they it's all in the past.
They say that it is not their burden,
And their debt no longer lasts.

They say that we are now treated equally.
They say let bygones go quietly by.
They say the past does not reflect the present,
But we all know that is a blatant lie.
They say they acknowledge the wrong doings.
They say that we are now back on track.
They say that there is now transparency,
But won't give our stolen artefacts back.

They say colonialism was a stain on history.
They say those were different times.
They say they are not accountable,
Yet still benefit from despicable crimes.
They say so many ludicrous things
In order to absolve their guilt,
But they can't hide from their barbaric history,
Of which their rich nations were built.

Woke

The spotlight is upon us,
Everyone is suddenly woke,
To the harrowing cries of black people,
Who weren't listened to when we spoke.

We told you about our struggles,
But many were quick to discard,
Thinking that we were exaggerating,
Playing the elusive race card.

We never wanted handouts,
This has obviously been misheard.
We don't want preferential treatment,
Just for our voices to be clearly heard.

We are more than capable.
Of achieving remarkable things,
If we're afforded equal privileges,
Without the attachment of conditional strings.

The right to be treated,
Without judgements and assumptions,
Unfair stereotypes,
That lead to false presumptions.

It’s great that so many people,
Have started to realise,
That our stories were not fictional,
But factual with painful cries.

So now the woke are aware,
Of our trials and tribulations.
Let’s see if there is a united effort,
To repair this divided nation.

My Smile

Please don't be fooled
By the smile on my face.
It rarely equates to happiness
But a way to erase,
The frustration deep inside
Of which I've been conditioned to hide,
So instead I gently smile
Whilst knowing all the while
That the pain of which I feel,
Will never be understood
When I constantly see images
Of all the things that should
Horrify every conscience,
Moisten every eye,
Calling those to action
To start to question why
We turn a convenient blind eye,
Allowing injustice to fly,
Far away, far from sight
Like a bird in mid flight.

Pretending things have not been seen
Trying to wipe racist surfaces clean.
So on days when I smile
And you think everything's okay,
I'm merely coping
Day by day,
As my mind drifts away
To the cries of my people
Whose suffering still remains,
As mental slavery takes hold
And our mind is still in chains.

So I smile,
Not because I'm content
But in order to cope
For it is just a pretense,
That is always at my expense
Which to you
Probably makes no sense,
So I smile to stay alive.
I smile each day to survive
For when my smile
Turns into a frown,
My heart will embrace revenge
And slowly drown.

White Fragility

Afraid of what we say
So as not to offend.
Tiptoeing over every word
When will this ever end?
We need to release.
We need to speak
Some uncomfortable truths
With a high-pitched shriek.

We often hold back.
We often protect
Those who rarely show us
The same respect.
Softening our words,
We're conditioned and prone
To appease white fragility
By softening our tone.

Fearful of causing them
Any signs of distress,
Stumbling to articulate
So with our words we caress.
We soothe their conscience.
We cuddle their shame.
We nurture their fragility.
We support their delicate frame.

As we cater to their needs
So we are not seen as a threat,
But they never show the same courtesy
And are quick to forget,
That when we are the subject
Our feelings are never considered.
They never have to question
How their words are delivered.

Angry Black Woman

Depicted as angry, as bitter and cold.
Defensive and defiant,
Never doing as we're told.

Depicted as bossy, confrontational and loud.
Too argumentative
And definitely too proud.

Depicted as difficult, always in a bad mood.
Stubborn and uppity, arrogant and rude.

Depicted as divas, bad-tempered and challenging.
Head-rocking, finger-waving.
These terms are so damaging.

Is this how we're defined? No, I think not!
So let me change the narrative,
In case you forgot.

Depicted as strong, courageous and brave.
Resilient and fearless, no longer a slave.

Depicted as confident, determined and smart.
Compassionate and loyal
With a tender, loving heart.

Depicted as freethinking, independent
and driven.
Overcoming countless obstacles
Of which we've been given.

Depicted as inventive, creative and inspiring.
Consistent trendsetters,
Leaving others admiring.

So I hope that I've set the record straight.
Don't ever call me angry
Unless you can relate.

You couldn't walk in my shoes,
not even for a mile.
Yet still I persevere with a courteous smile.

So if you're not a black woman
But understand the things we've been through,
Just maybe, sometimes,
You should be angry too.

Black Faces

I remember a time,
When we would hardly see,
Any black faces,
On the TV.
If there was a black family,
On a TV quiz show,
We would ring all of our friends,
So that everyone would know.

We'd switch over channels,
So eager to see,
Faces that looked black,
Just like me.
We'd get a few shows,
And feel elevated,
But there was never enough,
Leaving us thoroughly frustrated.

Do you remember,
No Problem and Empire Road?
We'd tune in and watch,
Every episode.
There was also Desmond's,
And the Real McCoy.
Tears of laughter,
And much needed joy.

We also had The Crouches,
And The Lenny Henry Show.
It seemed as if diversity,
Was starting to grow.
But we need more black writers,
We have stories to tell,
That should come from our voices,
Because only WE know us well.

We've come a long way,
From minstrel shows,
But still we've got
Much further to go.
Many of our actors,
Have to go overseas,
To get decent roles,
And that simply shouldn't be.

We've got so much talent,
That deserves to be seen.
Not hidden away,
From our TV screens.
It's time for the studios,
To heavily invest,
So our lack of representation,
Can be truthfully addressed.

Message In The Music

Music is expression.
It's poetry in motion.
Able to inspire us,
Tapping into our emotions.
Many of our musical legends,
Did more than simply sing.
There was a message in their music,
That their voices were destined to bring,

James Brown told the world,
'I'm black and I'm proud!'
He encouraged his people,
To sing it out loud.
This became our anthem,
To instill forgotten pride,
In our roots and our culture,
That many wanted us to hide.

Sam Cooke beautifully told us
That a change was gonna come.
He envisioned a time
When our suffering would be done.
Marvin Gaye asked the question,
'What's going on?'
As his people were in turmoil,
For centuries too long.

Nina Simone wanted to know,
How it would feel to be free,
And used her charismatic voice,
To highlight inequality.
She sang about Mississippi,
After terrible crimes,
To ensure that such atrocities,
Would never leave our minds.

Many more artists,
Have used the stage,
To sing out to people,
And express their rage.
They are more than just singers,
They were courageous and strong.
Bold enough to sing,
About the system that was wrong.

So whenever you hear their songs,
Listen to their every word.
There is a message in their music,
That should never go unheard.

Don't Touch My Hair

Please be aware,
Don’t ask to touch my hair.
I’m not an artefact,
So let's make a simple pact,
That you won't ask me again
From this question you'll refrain.
I hope you understand,
That your hands are always banned,
So please don’t even dare,
To attempt to touch my hair.

Please be aware,
Don’t ask to touch my hair.
I wish you’d hear me clearly,
This is making me quite weary.
I don’t want to be abrupt,
Or get angry and erupt.
I don’t want to lose my cool,
So obey my simple rule.
You are always free to stare,
Just don’t ask to touch my hair.

Black Beauty

Your black skin is beauty,
So never be afraid,
Be proud of your complexion,
No matter the shade.
Whether your skin is fair,
Or whether it is dark,
Your skin simply ignites,
A dynamic spark.
To possess such powerful strength,
Embedded in your rich skin,
Is your undeniable power,
Magnanimous melanin.
So wherever you are,
It is your ultimate duty,
To flaunt your black skin,
You amazing black beauty.

African Acestory

I'm proud of my heritage,
I'm African by birth.
I am rich in African culture,
The forefathers of this earth.

I'm proud of my ancestors.
I'm African in my DNA,
I am blessed with genetic wonders.
This is the African way.

I'm proud to be African.
I'm dipped in lineage so grand.
I am African, first and foremost,
A descendant of the motherland.

Biased Perceptions

When we're confident,
It's seen as arrogance.
When we're opinionated,
They challenge our intelligence.
When we're indignant,
It's seen as negative.
When we oppose,
They say we're argumentative.
When we are unapologetic,
It's seen as defiant.
When we stand firm,
We're no longer compliant.

When we proceed
To ask difficult questions,
They'll try to shut us down,
With excuses and exceptions.
When we are articulate,
And have flair with our words,
They close their ears,
To the truth that they've heard.
So we need to continue,
To shatter misconceptions,
To rid the world,
Of biased perceptions.

Seconds

It only takes a few seconds,
To hold a knife.
It only takes a few seconds,
To take a life.
We stab one another
With zealous urgency,
Why are my brothers
So blind to see?
The knife has become
A deadly noose,
As they kill one another
And exchange abuse.

Fighting over areas
Which they don't own,
While the government sits back
And casually condone
As our men kill each other
With no value placed upon,
The life of a brother,
The life of someone's son.
Our ancestors had to suffer
Fleeing from persecution,
While our young men today
Carry out their own execution.

How many more tears
Must be unnecessarily shed?
How many more boys
Will end up dead?
Before they prosper,
Before they have matured,
When will they live a life
Where their safety is ensured?

Instead families grieve.
And have to contend
With crushing heartache
And pain that never ends.
This crisis is killing us.
It's rampant and it's rife.
We need to stop the murders,
And start to respect life.

When They See Us

When they see us,
What do they see?
People with equal status,
Or dregs of society?
Do they see our talents,
Our beauty, our shine?
Or do they see negativity,
In order to undermine?

Do they see our strengths,
Or simply view us as scum?
Or do they fear our resilience
As we still manage to overcome?
It really doesn't matter,
How others view us with their eyes.
It starts with knowledge of self.
With this spirit we will rise.

Blackonomy

To have our own businesses,
To build and invest.
To fend for ourselves,
Is the ultimate test.

To support one another.
Is where it all begins.
To utilise our spending power,
To work from within.

To trust each other.
To bond and unite.
To have a common goal,
With vision and foresight.

To stand together,
To all dig deeper.
To have our own blackonomy,
Our own financial keeper.

Justice

What does justice look like?
What should we be able to see?
A reformed judicial system
That represents people that look like me.

Different sentences given
Mainly based upon race.
Comparisons made are apparent
As justice vanishes without trace

A judiciary that is prejudiced
Heightens all our fears,
Alienated from a fair trial
And a jury of our peers.

A system designed to trap us,
Of which, we can not flee,
Entrapment and corruption,
Bargaining for a plea.

Money buys you freedom.
Poverty does not serve you well.
Lack of finances leaves one option,
No bail, stuck in a cell.

Judges with a racist mindset.
Sentences that don't fit the crime
Watching counterparts receive pardons,
While our people serve prolonged time.

So, what does justice look like,
It is just a big disguise,
Unless you look at justice,
Through a pair of privileged eyes.

Dear Karen

Dear Karen, please don't cry,
Wipe away your fragile tears.
It's time to fabricate a story,
To justify your baseless fears.

We know that your tears have value,
They are more precious than gold,
You deserve to be punished,
For all the wicked lies you've told.

But still we'll accommodate you,
Your words hold so much weight,
We'll always believe your story,
Even when it's derived from hate.

It must be such a privilege
To always be seen as the best.
To walk through life with a capital K
Written on your conceited chest.

You've always been placed on a pedestal,
Thinking you were the cream of the crop.
But you've always felt inferior.
Your entitled mask is starting to drop.

You believe that you are special,
More beautiful than one's imagination,
But your insecurity still lingers,
From the days on the plantation.

Your husbands worshipped your existence,
In public, you were their queen,
But late at night, as they raped their slaves,
You closed your eyes to things you'd seen.

So your hatred stems from the past,
And your privilege still remains,
In order to boost your ego,
You play the victim and inflict pain.

But the world's eyes have been opened,
They now see your dangerous game.
You are a master manipulator,
One who clearly has no shame.

Countless men were lynched,
Because of your wicked lies,
The past has shown your character,
So your actions are no surprise.

You still hold so much power,
You know your stories will be believed,
Recklessly using your privilege,
While others are left aggrieved.

But please don't panic, Karen,
I have tissues ready at hand,
So when your tears start to fall,
The world will understand.

Don't give up your acting class,
Practise your distressed voice,
Keep pretending that calling the police,
Was your only choice.

We'll always find an excuse for you,
We'll say you were off your medication,
That you're definitely not a racist,
And love all of God's creations.

You'll read out a fake apology,
And cry a few more tears,
And then your crimes will vanish,
They'll simply disappear.

Dear Karen, don't you worry,
Society will always have your back,
As long as you are white
And I am simply black.

Questions

My beautiful, dark skin,
This mesmerising, abundance of melanin,
Does it offend you,
And often incite rage?
This blessing of mine,
That rarely shows signs of age.

Does it bother you?
To see me walk with pride.
Would you rather I feel inferior,
Maybe bleach my skin or hide?

Does it disgust you?
Do you think I'm too dark?
Are you threatened by my confidence,
So you hurl racist remarks?

Does it frustrate you?
This dark skin, deemed as less than,
As you eagerly rush to the salon,
To imitate me and enhance your tan.

Does it annoy you?
So you instilled that lighter skin was alright,
Setting Eurocentric beauty standards,
To keep my dark skin out of sight.

Does it threaten you?
As my skin's radiance glistens,
When you told the world it was ugly,
I prevailed and did not listen.

Does it irritate you?
That when you try to look like me,
You burn and peel in the sun
While I glow effortlessly.

Does it upset you?
That your tan will always fade,
While my dark skin is magical,
It's natural, not man-made.

Does it awaken your curiosity.
About possessing such glorious skin?
As I strut around majestically,
Loving the sumptuous layers I'm wrapped
tightly in.

Does it make you question,
All the lies that you've been told?
That my skin was less desirable.
You've been brainwashed and controlled.

I’ve never sought your approval,
To believe in the beauty of my dark skin.
Instead, I stand proud and resilient,
Determined to shine and win.

Black Excellence

What is black excellence?
It's you and it's me,
Displaying our talents,
For everyone to see.

Black excellence is power.
Black excellence is resilience.
Dominating many fields,
With our undeniable brilliance.

Black excellence is inspiring.
Black excellence is strength.
Chasing our dreams,
By any means or lengths.

Black excellence is innovative.
Black excellence is pride.
Recognition of our achievements.
Gloriously magnified.

Black excellence is outstanding.
Black excellence is unstoppable.
Knocking down countless barriers,
To achieve the impossible.

Black excellence is dynamic.
Black excellence is breathtaking.
Being a role model,
For future stars in the making.

Black excellence is you.
Black excellence is me.
Striving to be,
The very best that we can be.

Proud to Be

I’m proud to be a black woman
With all that it entails.
My words are carried by the ocean
As the wind blows on my impressive sails.

I’m proud to be resilient
As I walk through life’s revolving doors,
Navigating through many swings and turns.
Victorious in many wars.

I’m proud to be a poet
With the ability to express
My inner thoughts and feelings
Releasing all my contained stress.

I’m proud to be ambitious
As I strive for more each day,
Paying homage to those before me
Those who bravely paved the way.

I’m proud to be black.
I love my culture and history.
I wouldn't change it for the world.
I’m proud just being me.

Not Our Grandparents

Our grandparents had to be humble,
They had to hold their tongue,
Their journey was harrowing,
Their efforts were unsung.

Our grandparents witnessed horrors,
That our eyes will never see,
Robbed of their civil rights,
And basic dignity.

Our grandparents withstood conditions,
That were poor and unfair,
So their children could do better,
And could proudly walk on air.

So we are not our grandparents.
We're not on the same wave length,
They deserve our full respect,
For their courage and their strength.

BLACK MAGIC

They call it Black Magic,
But there is no voodoo
To explain all of the excellence
In things that we do.
There is no magic
We're just gifted and blessed,
That's why we conquer
And strive for the best

We are not fictional.
We are not a magical spell.
We are resilient people,
Hence why we do so well.
They've tried to defeat us,
Tried to hold us back,
But despite their best efforts
We still rise while under attack.

We've challenged your laws.
We've withstood your brutality.
We've battled with institutional racism
And created our own reality.
We've knocked down your barriers.
We've shattered your lies.
We've risen to the top,
Much to your shocked surprise.

We've obliterated your stereotypes.
We've rocked you to your core.
We've been militant and resistance.
We won't be tolerated anymore.
We've more than proven
Our abilities are strong,
While your narrative is falsified
And your history is wrong.

We're amazing, we're outstanding.
We won't ever give in,
Because we are determined
And destined to win.
You can't resist our power.
You can't deny our talent.
Our people are wise,
Bold and gloriously gallant.

There's no better time
To show what we can do.
Stand up, stand tall,
We are many, not few.
So lets have faith in our abilities.
Go forth and believe
That united together
We will always achieve.

Brave

We've always been defined as strong.
We wear it as a badge of pride
But this never allows us to feel weak,
We endure sorrow and skillfully hide
The pain we feel deep inside,
With assumed thick skin,
Limiting our ability to be nurtured
Because our insecurities are shielded within.

We feel pain and we hurt.
Our skin ruptures and it bleeds
But who is there to soothe our wounds?
Who is there to cater to our needs?
It's easier to believe
That we don't feel any pain,
So our suffering is invisible
While the strong stereotype remains.

Let's redefine our title,
No longer strong, instead we are brave,
Dealing with so many of life's obstacles
With resilience in how we behave.
We cry tears that flow like rivers.
We feel pain like the wound of a gun.
We continue like injured soldiers.
While our hearts melt from the heat of the sun.

But where is our saviour?
At times we need a pair of caring hands
To shield us from our suffering,
One who truly understands
That we often cry in silence
From the trauma and the weight,
That the world dumps on our shoulders
But our rescuers arrive too late.

Allow us to be transparent.
Allow us to shed a tear.
Allow us to relinquish our strong title.
Allow us to express our inner fears.
Allow us to be vulnerable.
Allow us to sob until our tears run dry.
Allow us to release our anxieties.
Allow us to exhale and sigh.

When we are allowed to be fragile,
Like a normal human being.
We can be true to our authentic selves.
This will be truly freeing.
It's time to take off our masks
Before we go to our sacred graves,
Standing proudly in the knowledge
That we are simply brave.

Colour Blind

If you don't see my colour,
Then surely you are blind.
My colour is the first thing,
That comes into your mind.
I was born in this colour.
Of this, I had no control.
I am proud of who I am.
My colour is my soul.
It is not a badge of shame,
I embody all of its glory.
My colour has its own narrative
Boldly telling its own story.
No need to shy away from my colour,
Open your eyes and clearly see,
This colour that shines so brightly,
Is unapologetically me.

Black

I love being black,
There's nothing that I lack,
From my skin to my hair,
I am fully aware,
That I have been blessed,
Despite being oppressed.
Anointed with melanin,
Warrior spirit deep within,
To withstand the struggle,
When I am forced to juggle,
All that life throws at me,
With courage and dignity.
But no matter how much I'm held back,
My spirit won't crack.
I love being black.

Invisible

It seems as if we've been invisible,
Which seems extremely weird
As we have always been here
But suddenly our faces have appeared,
Ticking many boxes
On inclusion and diversity lists,
But why now the sudden interest
To verify that we exist?

Inundated with black presenters.
They're popping up all over the screen.
Where have they been hiding?
Why have they never previously been seen?
Nearly every advert
Has someone that is black,
Or racially ambiguous
To fill in all the cracks.

Have the powers that be
Had vision that was impaired?
Now they can see clearly
So black faces can be declared.
Why all the sudden interest?
Is it part of their diversity training?
It does not feel very genuine,
Because for years we've been complaining.

Our Hair

Our hair is unique,
With a radiant glow.
Curls tightly coiled,
In a majestic fro.
Whether it's teeny weeny,
Or mammoth in size,
Our hair attracts attention,
And dazzles curious eyes.

Our hair is phenomenal.
Our hair embodies strength.
Our hair is not defined,
By the measurement of length.
Rejecting the notion,
That our hair is undesired.
Showcasing natural hair,
So young girls can be inspired.

Let's embrace our hair.
We don't need Eurocentric validation.
It's time to stand in our own image,
For an Afrocentric celebration.
Walking with confidence.
Not trying to hide,
Our natural hair,
As we walk regally with pride.

Reclaiming our power.
Reclaiming our hair.
Reclaiming our beauty.
The bold always dare,
To ignore the beauty standards,
That have been unfairly set.
To diminish our presence.
Our confidence is a threat.

A threat to the system,
That has tried to hold back,
Our beauty, our hairstyles,
Because we are black.
Brainwashing us to believe,
That our hair is too coarse,
But with deep love of self,
We are now back on course.

We will no longer allow,
You to regulate our hair.
Our hair represents power,
So we no longer care,
To adhere to your rules.
We now make our own.
We're proud of our hair,
So leave us alone.

Tired

Tired of explaining
All of the things we go through.
Tired of explaining
Things you already know are true.

Tired of explaining
Systemic racism set in place.
Tired of explaining
Why everything is about race.

Tired of explaining
What others should or should not say.
Tired of explaining
The same thing day after day.

Tired of explaining
That it's not my job to educate you.
Tired of explaining
That you can research information too.

Tired of explaining
Why I get so mad.
Tired of explaining
The tribulations my ancestors had.

Tired of explaining
Why the system is wrong.
Tired of explaining
That I'm tired of being strong.

Tired of explaining
That I don't have a bad attitude.
Tired of explaining
That I’m frustrated not rude.

Tired of explaining
About white fragility.
Tired of explaining
About my reality.

Tired of explaining
How racism affects my life.
Tired of explaining
All of my experiences and strife.

Tired of explaining
Racism to you.
We’re all so tired of explaining
That the solution lies with you.

Beauty

I define my own beauty.
I stand proud as a queen.
My aura shimmers; my stance is supreme.

I define my own beauty.
Not afraid to embrace
My natural complexion, no mask on my face.

I define my own beauty.
I always ensure to showcase my real features,
No need to contour.

I define my own beauty.
I may not always turn heads
But I embody a radiance that sparkles instead.

I define my own beauty.
My skin glistens in the sun
With a melanin explosion, I bow down to no one.

I define my own beauty.
Loving God's creation.
Boldly walking through life with leaps of
celebration.

I define my own beauty.
My nose is brilliantly broad
No plastic surgery because I'm no fraud.

I define my own beauty.
I know that I'm blessed
Even on days when I don't look my best.

I define my own beauty,
With all of my flaws
Being my own cheerleader, creating my own applause.

I define my own beauty,
Which at times causes shock
As my hair is not straight but instead I wear locs.

I define my own beauty,
Not trying to fit in.
I accept who I am in my glorious skin.

I define my own beauty.
I'm not desperate to be
A carbon copy of most faces that you always see.

I define my own beauty.
I'm not everyone's cup of tea
But I'm confident in who I am and I'm happy
being me.

I define my own beauty.
I walk proudly with my scars.
My stretch marks reflect my colourful
memoirs.

I define my own beauty.
I'm God's masterstroke,
Crafted by design, uniquely bespoke.

I define my own beauty.
My confidence is inspired,
For with my type of beauty,
No filter is required.

Twice as Good

We were always told
We had to be better than the best.
Mediocre wasn't an option,
Unlike all the rest.
We would have to work harder
Just to get our foot in the door.
We could not afford to be average,
Or we'd get the shortest straw.
So we did all we could
Then watched in distress,
As people less talented,
Continued to progress.

Realising that the playing field
Was not as equal as we assumed.
Our hard work was never enough.
It seemed that we were doomed.
Racism reared its ugly head
To keep our talents at bay,
Being sidelined for promotions,
So many of us lost our way.
But still we persevered
Knowing that we would come up short,
Frustrated by a lack of equity,
And all the battles that we fought.

So where are we today?
Has anything really changed?
Or has racism been repackaged
And conveniently exchanged,
For acts of disingenuous tokenism
Where our faces are more widely seen.
But the management structures of most companies,
Are still as white as they've always been.
Protecting their power,
Still maintaining the status quo.
Recruitment isn't always about your talent
But based on who you know.

But there is an easy solution,
And this fact is very well known.
We need to be self-reliant,
And start businesses of our own.
When we fend for ourselves,
We'll no longer have to wait,
To be seen as second best.
And then we can dictate
Our own path and destiny
Building our own strong foundation,
Free from bigotry and bias,
No more need for their validation.

Profitable

We've always been profitable
From the time that we were enslaved.
Used and abused for our labour
With acts that were depraved.

Made to feel inferior
In a world that was not right,
Where standards were judged purely
On the glory of being white.

Our lives had no value.
We were always ridiculed,
About our distinctive features
But we were truly fooled.

Because all along they've wanted
All the things that we possess,
While making us believe
That what we had was so much less.

They laughed at our dark skin.
They laughed at our thick lips.
They laughed at our hairstyles
And our curvaceous hips.

They mocked our intelligence.
They mocked everything we did,
But deep inside they felt inferior
Of which they cleverly hid.

So now it seems these same features
Are marketable and desired.
Their belief of superiority
Has gloriously backfired.

The allure to look ambiguous,
As they casually adopt and steal
The aesthetics of marginalised black women
To widen their mass appeal.

They want to adopt our features.
They want to adopt our style.
They want to adopt our culture,
But only for a profitable while.

When it is lucrative,
They all want a piece of black
But when racial struggles appear
They rush to give it back.

We are not a seasonal trend
Or a fancy dress costume.
We're not an item in a store
That you can casually consume.

The whole world wants to police
Our bodies, complexions and hair,
While you can adopt the same styles
Without a single thought or care.

So you profit from our pain.
You profit at our expense,
Yet when we call you out on it
You find a quick defence.

Claiming that you love our culture
Is predictable and always said,
But have you ever spoken up for black issues?
Or have you conveniently been silent instead?

In this unjust world
I have only one wish,
We should tax repeat offenders
Whenever they blackfish.

Can't Hold Us Back

There ain't no black in the union jack,
A phrase we used to hear.
But there's no getting rid of us,
We just won't simply disappear.
We're here and we're not playing,
And we're not going to hide,
The way we feel about injustice,
Our voices are now amplified .

Refusing to turn a blind eye,
To racism on any level.
Not afraid of any reprisals,
Being a revolutionary rebel.
Holding others accountable,
For their actions and bigoted words.
Refusing fake apologies,
And pretending things haven't been heard.

No longer craving acceptance,
No longer trying to fit in,
By changing our natural appearance,
And hiding who we are within.
Boldly wearing our natural hair,
A rejection of trying to be,
Someone that were clearly not,
Adhering to conformity.

Being proud of our black features,
Our bodies and our roots.
Speaking out against discrimination.
No need for us to be mute.
Raising our black children,
To be proud of who they are.
Teaching them about their history,
Making sure they raise the bar.

Ensuring that they have a solid education,
And a clear knowledge of self.
Starting our own businesses,
To create generational wealth.
So if there ain't no black in the union jack,
We've truly come along way.
Persevering through adversity,
Refusing to be pushed away.

We've made so many outstanding
accomplishments,
And despite being seen as a threat,
We're here to stay, so trust me,
You ain't seen nothing yet.
We're exceeding all expectations,
We're embracing what it truly means,
To be a success on our own terms.
We're our ancestors' wildest dreams.

Teach Them

Black History is all around us,
Not just on allocated days.
Our contributions to society,
Have been tremendous in so many ways.
Our talents are often hidden,
So that negative stereotypes persist,
As if we have no major accolades,
Or our talents do not exist.

We've invented so many things,
That have changed the world we live in,
But rarely get any recognition,
And this is a terrible sin.
Our children deserve better.
It's up to us to make them aware,
Of all of the successful black people,
That surround them everywhere.

Those from the present,
Those from the past,
Those who are currently in the process,
Of making a legacy that will last.
We can't wait for the schools
To teach our children what they need to know.
It's time for us to step up,
And help our children to grow.

Teach them about self-love.
Teach them about ambition.
Teach them that despite any challenges,
Their dreams will come to fruition.
Teach them about black pride.
Teach them that they can win.
Teach them they are not inferior,
And to love the skin that they're in.

Teach them about their ancestors.
Teach them that they are kings and queens.
Teach them that they are invincible.
Even when others try to demean.
Teach them that they are special.
Teach them that they can succeed.
Teach them that they can conquer the world,
Becoming fearless and choosing to lead.

Black history is all round us,
So let's make sure that we're all sincere,
In teaching our children their history,
Every single day of the year.

Printed in Great Britain
by Amazon

68938826R00045